BIG STORY TREASURY

CHILDREN'S BOOKS

Contents

Lunar Fluffies

It was a shivery start to the day in Moona Luna.

A cup of hot cosmic cocoa for space adventurer Lunar Jim and Ripple, the engineer, was the most exciting thing to happen so far today.

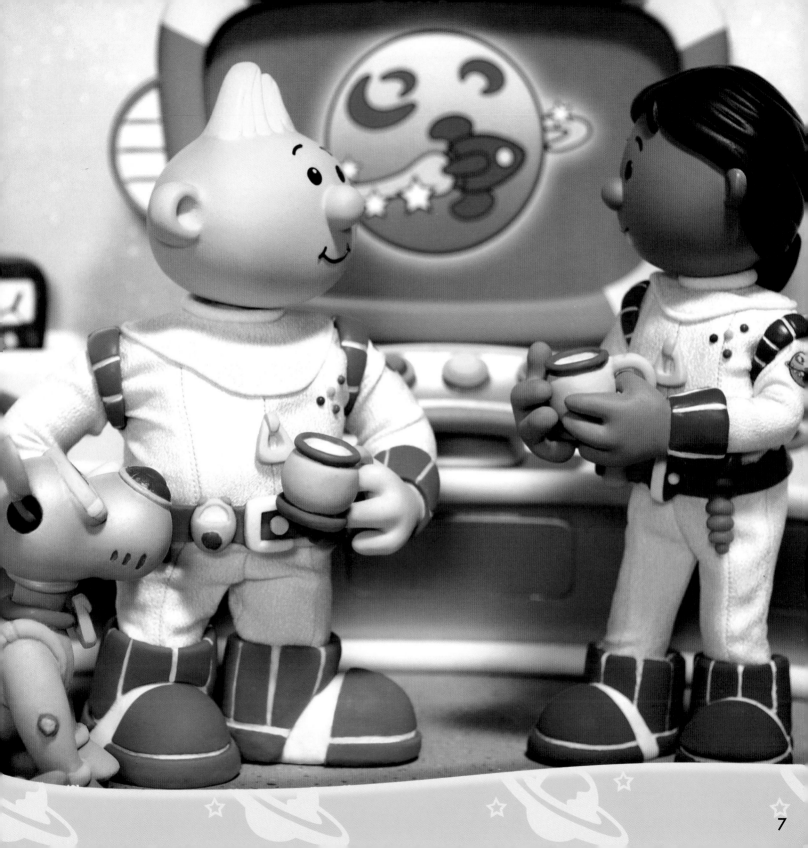

"Brrr... it's freezing!" shivered Jim, as Eco appeared on the View Comm.

"Jim, those crystals we collected yesterday give off heat as well as light!" cried Eco excitedly.

"We need more of those crystals right away!" shouted Jim. "Let's get lunar!"

T.E.D. was keen to get warm, so he went with Jim and Rover to find more crystals.

"I happen to be an expert at finding crystals, Jim," shivered T.E.D. "Especially if they are going to keep me warm!"

In the first cave they explored, Rover's bleeps and blips told them he'd found an interesting furry creature.

But T.E.D. insisted, "L-let's g-get to C-crystal C-cave b-before I t-turn into Icicle T-T.E.D.!

Strangely, as they left, the furry creature followed them...

Back at Mission Control, Ripple and Eco were delighted when the lunar explorers brought back plenty of new crystals.

While the others were busy warming themselves, Rover spotted the furry blue creature he'd seen in the cave.

"Ahhh! What's that? Save me!" squealed a terrified T.E.D. "Save my crystal, then save yourselves!"

Ripple picked up the cuddly creature with a smile. "I've always wanted a pet," she said, stroking it gently.
"I'm going to call it a Fluffy."

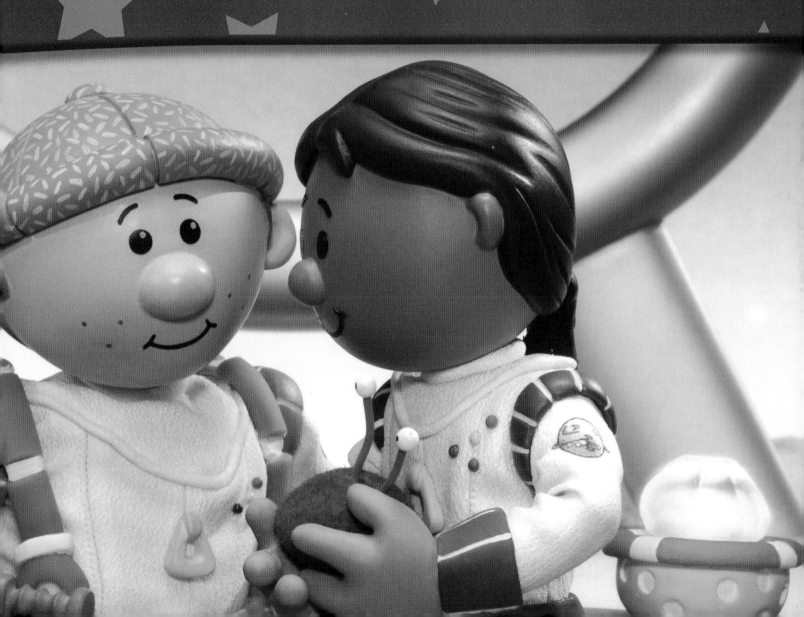

Next morning at the Ecodome, there were Fluffies everywhere!

"They must have appeared in the night," said Eco.

Jim was puzzled. "I wonder why the Fluffies came here?"

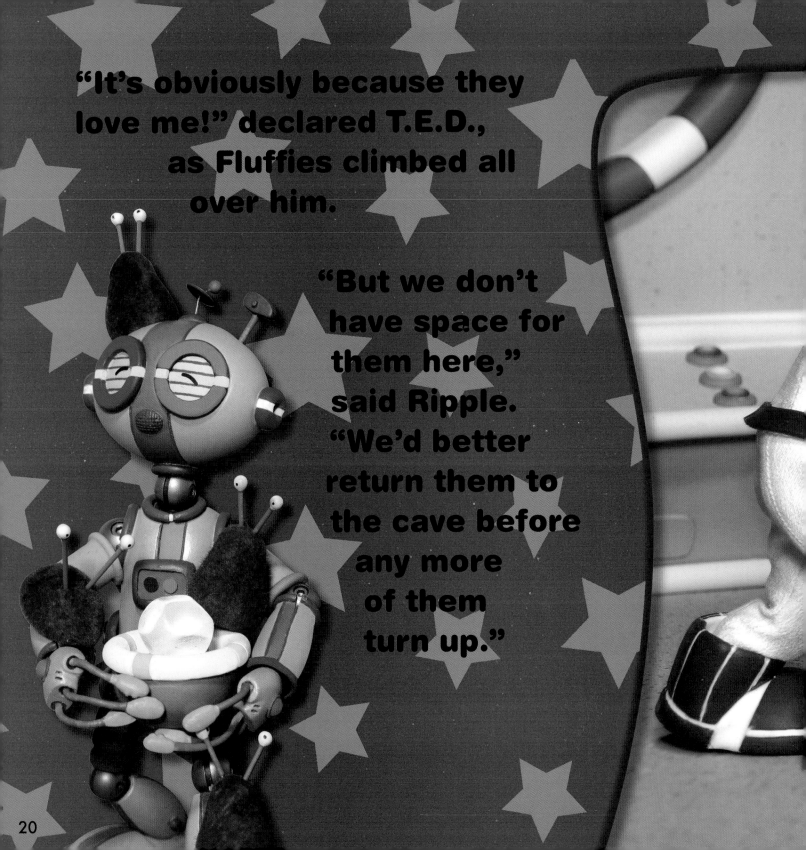

"It's obviously because they love me!" declared T.E.D., as Fluffies climbed all over him.

"But we don't have space for them here," said Ripple. "We'd better return them to the cave before any more of them turn up."

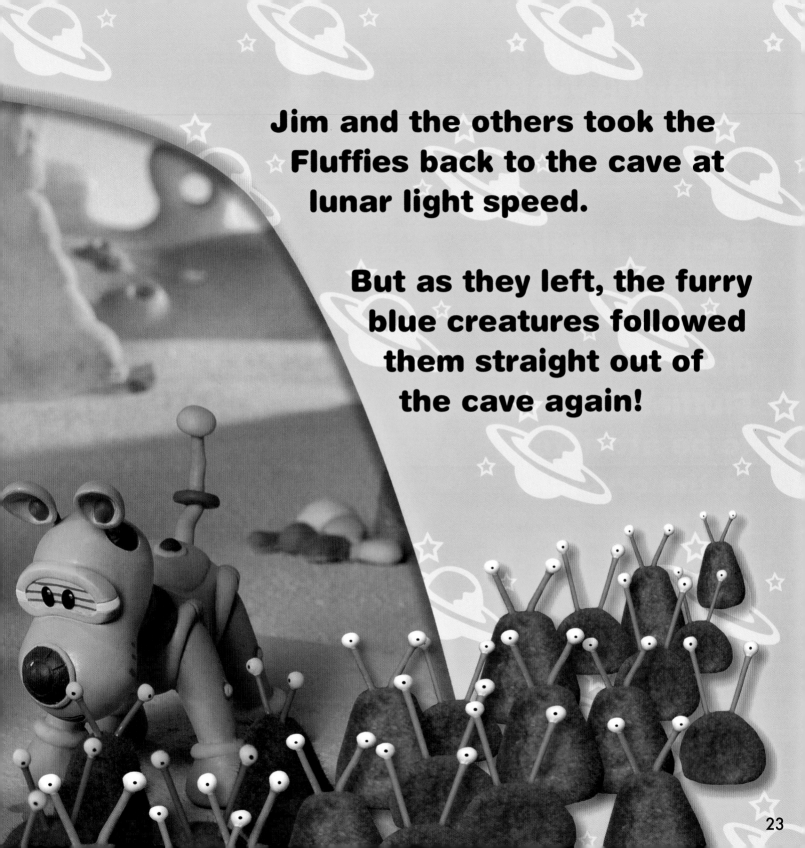

Jim and the others took the Fluffies back to the cave at lunar light speed.

But as they left, the furry blue creatures followed them straight out of the cave again!

"Jumping Jupiter," sighed Jim. "What do we do now?"

Back at Mission Control, T.E.D. was sad to discover that the Fluffies seemed to be attracted to the crystals, not him.

Suddenly, Jim understood the answer to their puzzle.

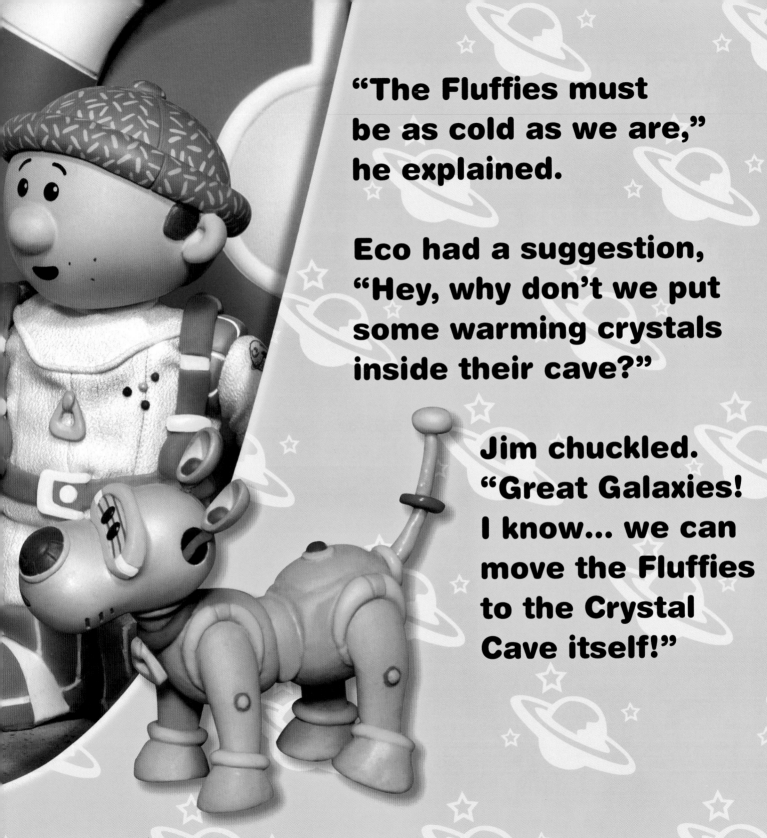

"The Fluffies must be as cold as we are," he explained.

Eco had a suggestion, "Hey, why don't we put some warming crystals inside their cave?"

Jim chuckled. "Great Galaxies! I know... we can move the Fluffies to the Crystal Cave itself!"

The Fluffies were very happy with their new home.

"It's a good thing Moona Luna winters only last for a few freezy days!" laughed Jim.

THE END

Tweenies™

Caterpillar Surprise

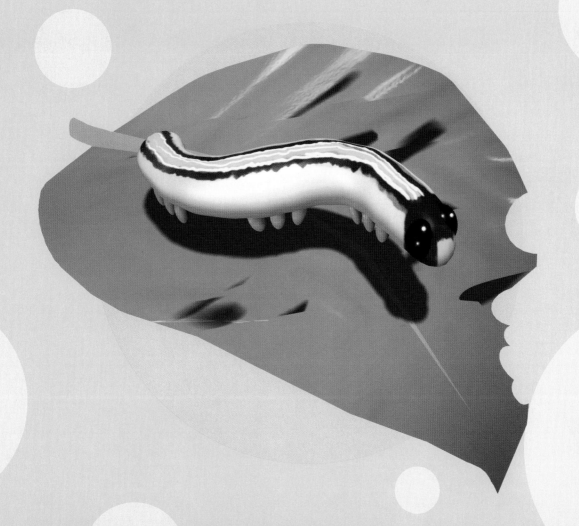

One day, Max went to visit a meadow. When he got back, the Tweenies wanted to know all about the things he had seen there.

"What did you see in the meadow, Max?" asked Fizz.
"Well, I saw some lovely wild flowers, some trees and lots of birds," Max replied.

"Did you bring anything back with you?" asked Milo.

"Do you know, I think I brought back some ants in my pants," replied Max, wriggling a bit.

That made Bella, Milo, Fizz and Jake giggle.

31

"What else did you see in the meadow, Max?" asked Jake.
"Did you see any tigers or elephants?" asked Milo.

"No, tigers and elephants don't live in meadows," Max explained. "But I made a video all about the bugs I saw. Shall we watch it together?"

Fizz pressed the button on the Tweenie clock.

"Telly time!" she shouted.

Then they all settled down in front of the telly.

33

"Look!" said Milo. "There's a spider."

"That's right," Max replied. "I saw lots of spiders."

"What's that creepy-crawly?" asked Jake, looking closely at the screen.

"That's a caterpillar, Jake. What else can you see?" asked Max.

"I can see a ladybird," said Fizz.

"Did you see any butterflies?" Bella asked. "I like butterflies."

"No, I didn't see any butterflies in the meadow today, Bella," replied Max.

"Oh," said Bella sadly.

"I know. Why don't we look for bugs in the garden?" suggested Max.

"Good idea, Max," agreed the Tweenies.

The Tweenies and Max went into the garden and
looked closely to see if they could spy anything
crawling under the bushes or munching on the leaves.

"I can't see anything," said Milo.

"Neither can I," said Fizz. "It's just trees and twigs
and grass."

"Oh, I can see something on that leaf," said Jake. "It looks like a jelly bean."

"That's not a jelly bean," said Bella. "It's a cocoon. There's a caterpillar inside it, and when it grows up it turns into something wonderful. We know a song about it... don't we, Max!"

39

Caterpillar walking,
Up and down the trees.

Caterpillar munching,
On the tasty leaves.

Caterpillar hiding,
Nowhere to be found.

Caterpillar sleeping,
Safe and sound.

"What happens next, Max?" asked
Milo. "Does the caterpillar wake up?"
"Well, Milo, the caterpillar does
wake up, in a way," replied Max.
"Let me explain."

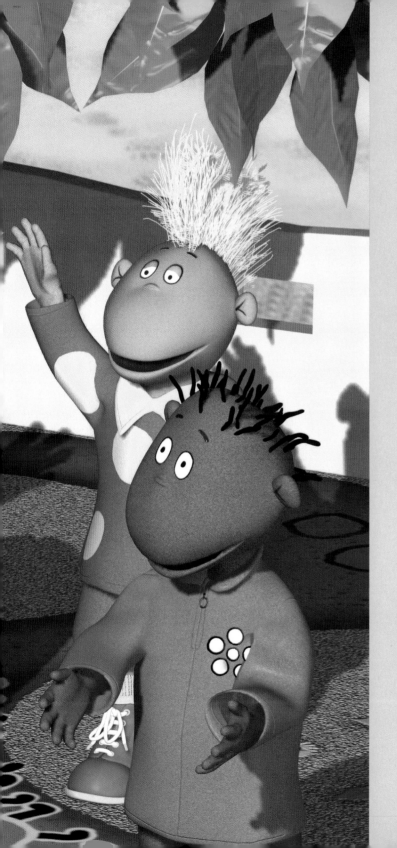

"First, a baby caterpillar grows from an egg. When the caterpillar gets bigger, it changes into something else."

"I know," said Bella. "The caterpillar changes into a..."

"Shhh, Bella!" said Max suddenly. "Let's keep the next bit a secret so that the change is a surprise."

"Can we take the cocoon inside?" asked Fizz.

"I think we should leave it here where it belongs. We can come and see it every day," replied Max.

Max went off to read the paper and the Tweenies went off to find different things to do.

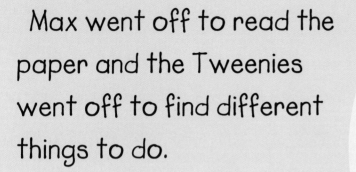

Jake painted a picture of a caterpillar and Fizz drew a picture of a ladybird. Bella read a book about butterflies.

But Milo started to wonder just what was going to happen when the caterpillar woke up.

45

Milo went outside
and peered under the leaf
at the cocoon. He thought
he saw it move, but nothing
much else happened.

"When are we going
to get our surprise?"
he wondered.

Then Fizz went outside
to see if anything had
happened to the cocoon,
but it still looked exactly
the same.

"Where's the surprise?"
thought Fizz.

Later, Jake went outside to see if the caterpillar had woken up yet. But all he could see was the little cocoon dangling from the leaf.

"It's not much of a surprise," thought Jake.

Only Bella stayed away from the garden. She knew that you had to be patient if you wanted to enjoy this surprise. She carried on reading her book. It had some lovely pictures in it.

The next day, the day after and the day after that, there was still no sign of the caterpillar waking up. Then, early one morning, Max called Bella into the garden.

The cocoon had broken open! The outsides of the caterpillar's silky coat fell to the ground. Something small and crumpled held on tightly to the leaf.

"Oh, Max, isn't it lovely?" smiled Bella, as the small crumpled thing opened up slowly and stretched its wings.

The other Tweenies came
out to see what it was.

"Oh, it's a flutterby!" cried Jake.

"You mean a butterfly," said Fizz.

"Wow, what a great surprise!" cried Milo.

"Now we can sing the rest of the song,
Max," said Bella.

50

Caterpillar waking,
Looks up at the sky

Opens out her wings,
And becomes a butterfly!

"Bye-bye butterfly!" The Tweenies waved goodbye to the beautiful butterfly as it fluttered away, over their heads and up, up, up into the sky.

THE END

Florrie's Flag

It was a lovely sunny day in Fimble Valley.

Florrie was helping Baby Pom
to build a tower,
and Fimbo and Rockit
were having races.

Just as Florrie put
the last block on
the top of Baby
Pom's tower,
she heard the
Tinkling Tree
tinkling.

"I'm getting the Fimbling
Feeling!" she cried.

"I can feel a twinkling,
I can hear a sound,
It's telling me there's something
Waiting to be found!
Where is it? Where is it?
What could it be?
I think it might be over there,
Let's go and see!"

Florrie's find looked like a black and white tablecloth stuck to a stick. She waved it in the air. Swoosh! Swoosh!

"Oooh, you've found a flag!" chirped Bessie. "A special flag! It's called a chequered flag. You wave it to finish a race."

"Fimbo and Rockit love races," said Florrie. "I'll go and wave my flag for them!"

All the racing they had done, though, had made Rockit and Fimbo very hungry.

And then all the apples and Crumble Crackers they had eaten had made them very sleepy...

Zzzzzzzzzzz...

"Fimbo, Rockit, wake up! Look what I've found!"
cried Florrie. "A special flag you use to finish a race."

"Fimbo! Glung! Want to race?" said Rockit.

Zzzzzzzzzzz...

"Never mind!" said Rockit. "I'll race Bessie and Roly instead."

"We'll start and finish the race here, by Pom's tower,"
said Florrie.

"I'm just going to go and eat an apple to give me lots of energy," said Rockit, bouncing off.

"You start without me. I'm so fast, I'll easily catch up with Bessie and Roly!"

"On your marks...

get set...

GO!" shouted Florrie.

And Bessie and
Roly Mo were off!

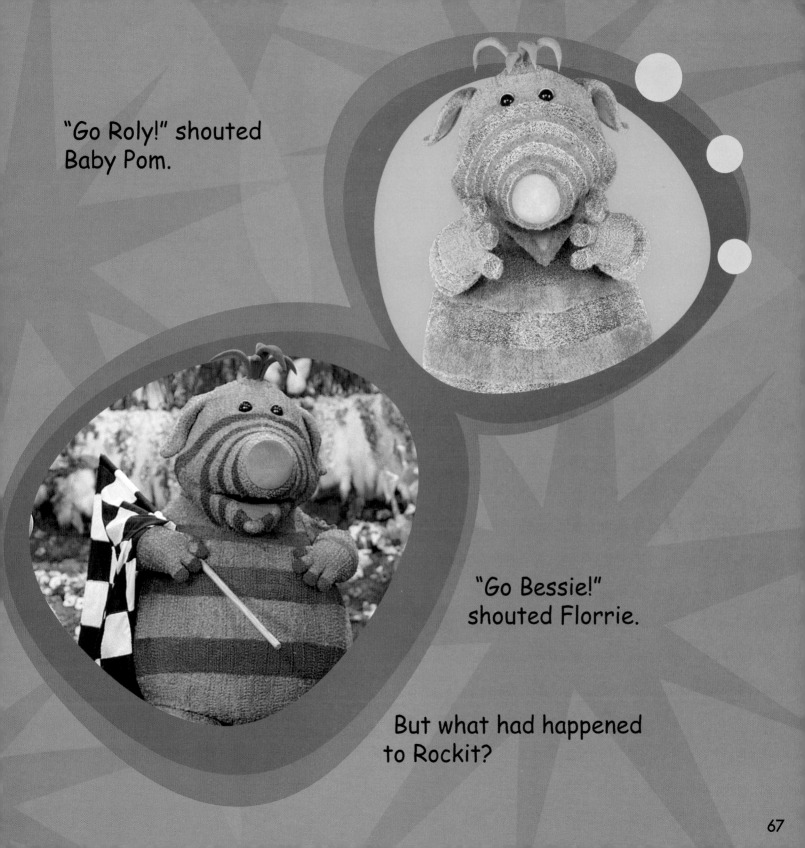

"Go Roly!" shouted Baby Pom.

"Go Bessie!" shouted Florrie.

But what had happened to Rockit?

67

Eating an apple had made Rockit sleepy all over again.

Zzzzzzzzzz...

Baby Pom and Florrie's shouting
woke Rockit up.

"Glung!" he glunged, bouncing off the Comfy Corner.
"Oh no! The race!"

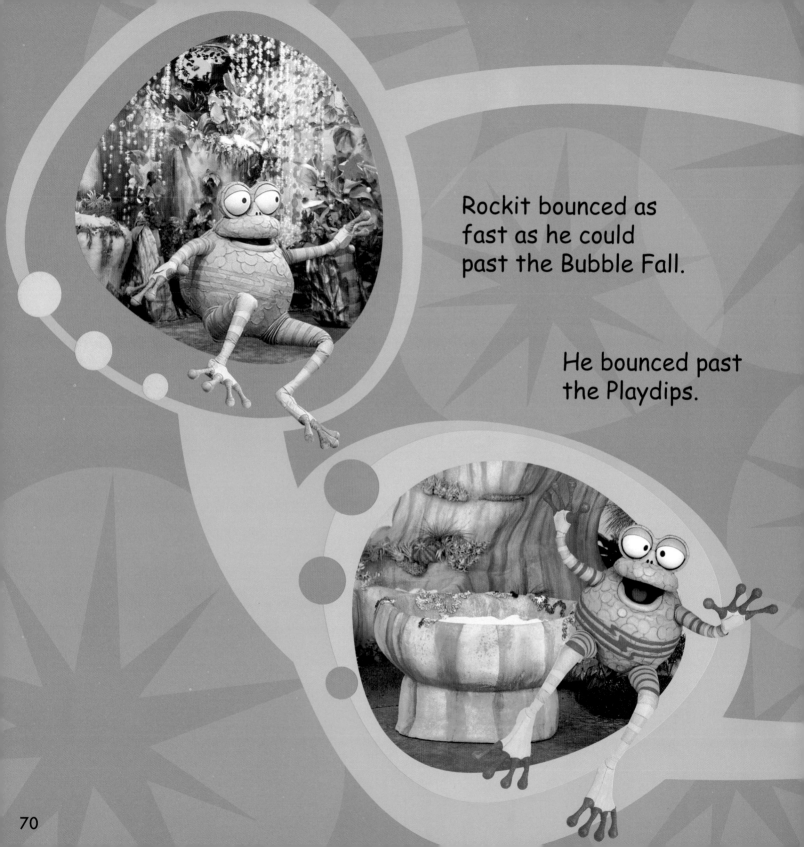

Rockit bounced as
fast as he could
past the Bubble Fall.

He bounced past
the Playdips.

He bounced past the
Tinkling Tree.

He bounced as he had never
bounced before.

At the finish line, Florrie was holding her flag.

Bessie fluttered past.

"Bessie's first," she cried. Swoosh! went the flag.

Roly rolled past.
"Roly's second," she cried. Swoosh!

Rockit bounced in at
top speed...

...straight into Baby Pom's tower. CRASH!

"Rockit's third!" Florrie laughed. Swoosh!

"Tickle my tadpoles! That was fun, even though I didn't win!" said Rockit.

"What's going on?" yawned Fimbo, "I'm ready for more races now. Anyone want to race?"

"Yes!" shouted everyone.
Swoosh! went Florrie's flag.

The Tubby Custard Mess

One day in Teletubbyland, it was time for tubby custard.

But then Dipsy had an accident.

Uh-oh! Dipsy spill tubby custard.

Dipsy spilt tubby custard all
over his tubby seat.

Tinky Winky, Laa-Laa and Po sat down on their tubby seats. But Dipsy didn't want to sit down.

Dipsy didn't want to sit in the tubby custard.

Dipsy had nowhere to sit.
So Laa-Laa let Dipsy sit on her tubby seat.

But then Laa-Laa had nowhere to sit.
Laa-Laa didn't want to sit in the tubby custard.

Eeeeeyyyyrrrr!

So Po let Laa-Laa sit on her tubby seat.

But then Po had nowhere to sit.
Po didn't want to sit in the tubby custard.

So Tinky Winky let Po sit on his tubby seat.

But then Tinky Winky had nowhere to sit.
Tinky Winky didn't want to sit
in the tubby custard.

Dipsy and Laa-Laa
wanted Tinky Winky
to sit on their tubby seats.

Tinky Winky couldn't decide which tubby seat to sit on.

Po had an idea. She ran around
and sat on another tubby seat.

Tinky Winky sat next to her. But then
Dipsy and Laa-Laa wanted to sit down.

Dipsy and Laa-Laa tried to share a tubby seat.

parp
parp

But there wasn't room!

So Po stood up again.

Dipsy and Laa-Laa both tried to sit on Po's tubby seat.

parp parp

But there wasn't room!

Dipsy sat down on the tubby seat and Laa-Laa had nowhere to sit.

So Laa-Laa sang a song.
Tinky Winky, Dipsy and Po joined in.

sucky
slurpy
slurpy

While they were
singing, the
Noo-noo tidied up.

Now all the Teletubbies had somewhere to sit. But they were all sitting on the wrong tubby seats!

So the Teletubbies changed places...

again... and again... and again...

until they were all sitting in the right places.
And then it was time for tubby custard.

Teletubbies love tubby custard.
And Teletubbies love each other very much.

Big hug!

Lost and Found

Eco, the space farmer in Moona Luna, had a special surprise for his friends.

"No peeking," Eco told Lunar Jim, Rover, Daisy and Dolores.

"It's a..."

"...hand-knitted jumper to keep Daisy warm on these chilly lunar nights!" he declared proudly.

"It's lovely! But... isn't it a bit small?" asked Jim.

Eco had to agree. "All my knitting is wasted," he sighed loudly.

When Eco saw how sad Daisy looked, he promised to knit her a bigger jumper.

Rover put on the small jumper. It fitted him perfectly! He was delighted, and bleeped and blipped happily.

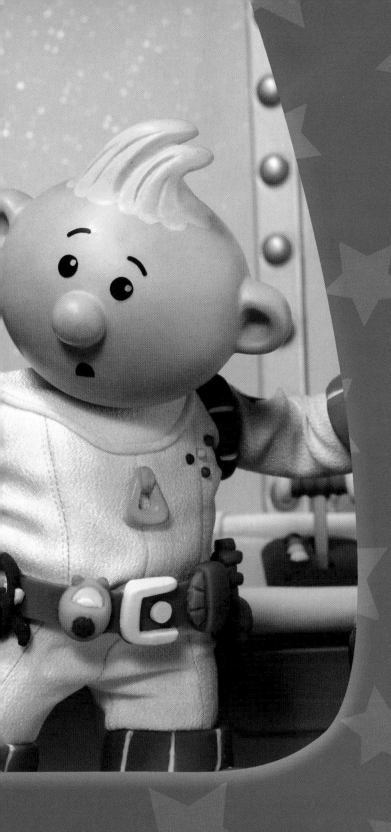

Jim, Rover and Eco went over to Mission Control to show off the new jumper, but Ripple and T.E.D. were nowhere to be found.

"Hmmm, that's strange," said Jim. "They should be back from their mission by now."

Meanwhile, Rover had got tangled up in a loose thread of his new jumper!

Just then, the big viewing
screen of the View Comm
blinked on.

"Hi Jim," said Ripple. "T.E.D.
and I got a bit... lost... in Nebula
Cave."

"Don't worry, Ripple, we're on our way!" Jim cried. "Let's get lunar!"

He and Rover jumped into the transport tube and, faster than lunar light speed, they were dressed in their space gear.

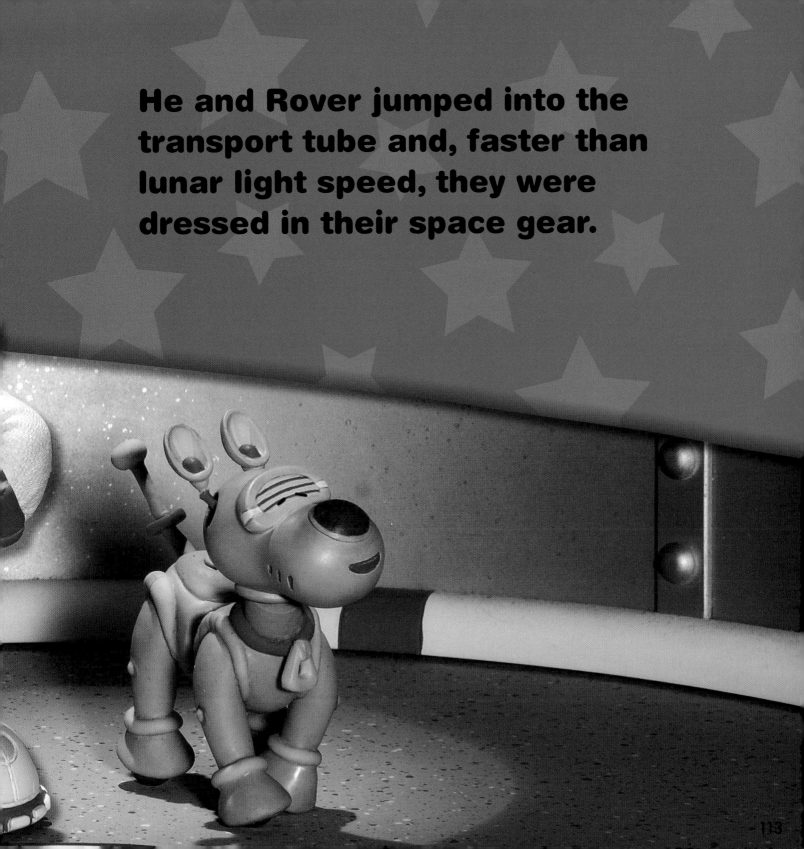

Jim chose the Lunar Hopper, a moon buggy big enough for Eco to join them in their search and rescue mission.

"Crashing Comets, here we come!" called Jim, as they bounded across the rocky surface of Moona Luna.

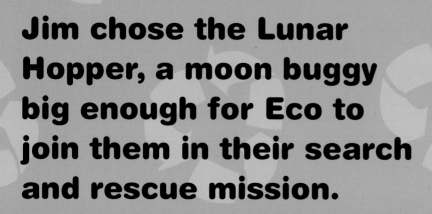

Deep inside Nebula Cave, T.E.D. was feeling really scared. "There might be moon bats, and space snakes, and..."

Ripple tried to calm her friend. "Don't worry, T.E.D., help is on its way."

"But how will they find us?" he whimpered.

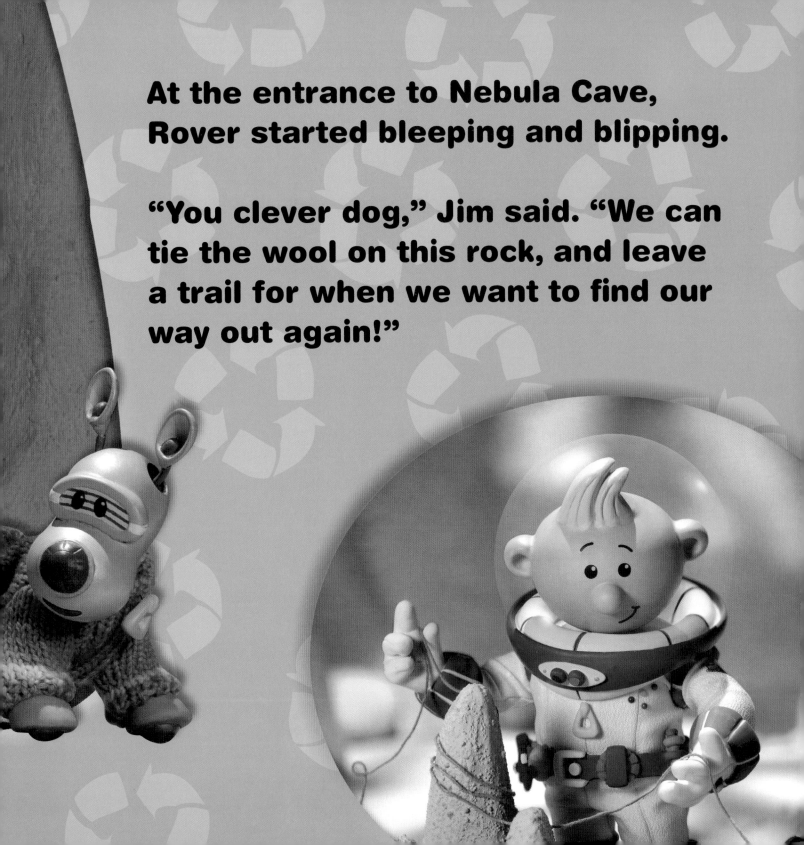

At the entrance to Nebula Cave, Rover started bleeping and blipping.

"You clever dog," Jim said. "We can tie the wool on this rock, and leave a trail for when we want to find our way out again!"

The wool idea
worked perfectly,
although the jumper
Eco had knitted
was almost gone by the
time they found their
lost friends in the middle
of Nebula Cave.

"Thanks for rescuing us,"
said Ripple.

But T.E.D. was still
panicking. "Help!
How can we find
our way out?"

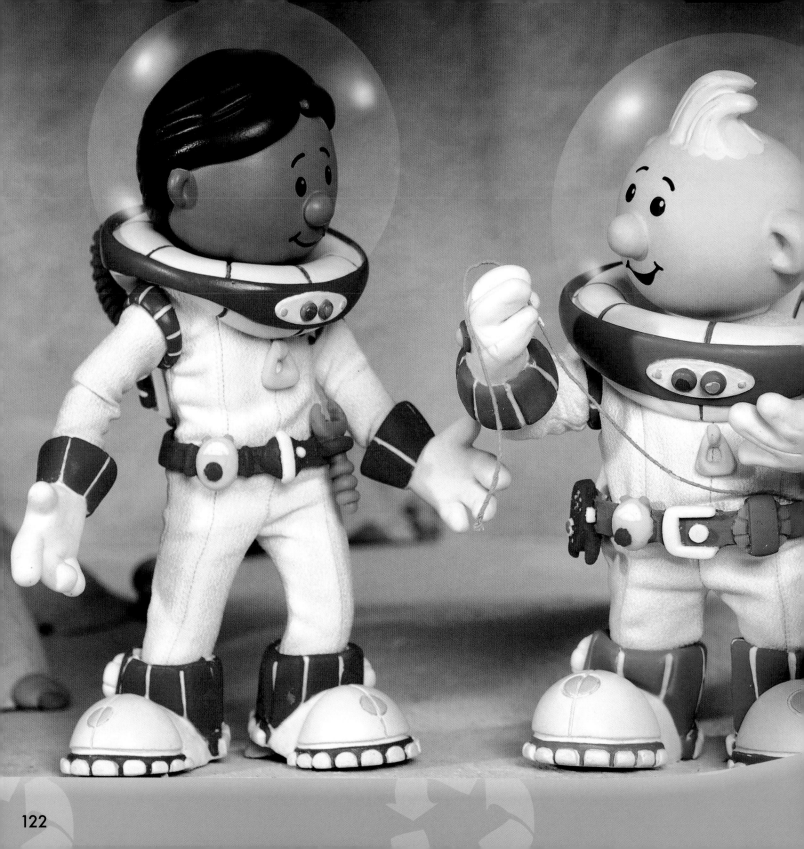

"Never fear, T.E.D., the trail is clear!" laughed Jim. And, using the wool as a guide, they made their way back to the cave entrance.

123

"So now I have two jumpers to make,"
said Eco, as he wound up the wool. "One
for Daisy, and a new one for Rover."

"It's a good job you like knitting!"
chuckled Jim.

THE END

Tweenies™
Happy Birthday, Fizz!

It was Fizz's birthday and as a special treat, Judy
had taken her to see a real ballet. While they were
out, Max helped Bella, Milo and Jake wrap up their
presents. Doodles watched. He liked birthdays.

"Can I ever have a birthday present?" Jake asked Max.

"Of course you can," Max replied.

"Oh, good!" said Jake, and helped himself to the biggest one!

"No, Jake!" cried Bella. "You can have a present on YOUR birthday. Today is Fizz's birthday so SHE gets the present!"

Max told the Tweenies that
birthdays were extra-special
days. Not only did you get
presents but you were also
another year older.

"Fizz is FOUR years old
today," he told them.

The Tweenies helped Max
get ready for the party.
Milo found the party hats
and hung up the streamers.

Bella blew up the balloons and
Jake helped Max set the table.

129

When everything was ready, they made Fizz a birthday card with a big number four on the front.

"I've got a great idea," said Milo. "Why don't we stick four candles on Fizz's birthday cake?"

"Oh, yes!" cried Jake.

"OH, NO!" gasped Bella. "We haven't got a cake for Fizz. We forgot her cake!"

131

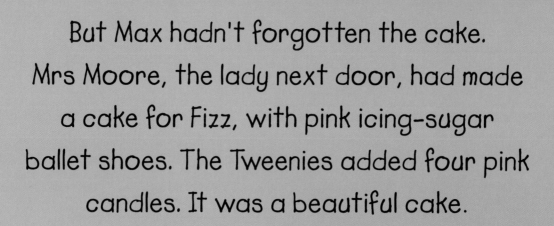

But Max hadn't forgotten the cake.
Mrs Moore, the lady next door, had made
a cake for Fizz, with pink icing-sugar
ballet shoes. The Tweenies added four pink
candles. It was a beautiful cake.

"What a shame it won't last," said Milo.

"Why won't it last?" asked Jake.

"Because we're going to EAT it, matie!" giggled Milo.

Max told the Tweenies that they couldn't eat the cake until Fizz had blown out the candles and made her birthday wish.

"Oh, I wish I could wish," sighed Jake.

"What would you wish for?" asked Max.

"Something really big and exciting," he replied.

"I know what I'd wish for," said Milo, and he made up a song about it...

"I wish I had a wish,
'cos then I'd wish
for a robot to play
in the park with me!"
he sang.

"I wish I had a wish,
'cos then I'd wish
for a star to dance in the sky
with me! **sang Bella.**

"I wish I had a wish,
'cos then I'd wish
for a dragon to come
and live with me!"
sang Jake.

"I wish I had a wish,
'cos then I'd wish
for sausages
with chops and gravy for
my tea!"

sang Doodles.

139

When Fizz came back with Judy, she was thrilled to see her party decorations. "I can't wait to start my party!" she cried, and went to hang up her coat.

Then Fizz noticed the pink icing-sugar ballet shoes on the cake.

"What BEAUTIFUL ballet shoes! I wish..." she began.

But it was time to open the presents.

Bella gave her a jigsaw and
Milo gave her a box of
coloured crayons.

"Guess what *my* present is," said Jake.
The parcel felt soft and squishy. Inside was a big packet
of jelly babies.

"Thank you, Jake," Fizz said. "We can all share them."

Next, Fizz opened a present
from Max and Judy. It was a
song book and a tape.

"We can all sing along
together," said Fizz.

When Judy lit the candles on the birthday cake, Max said he knew exactly which song they should sing.

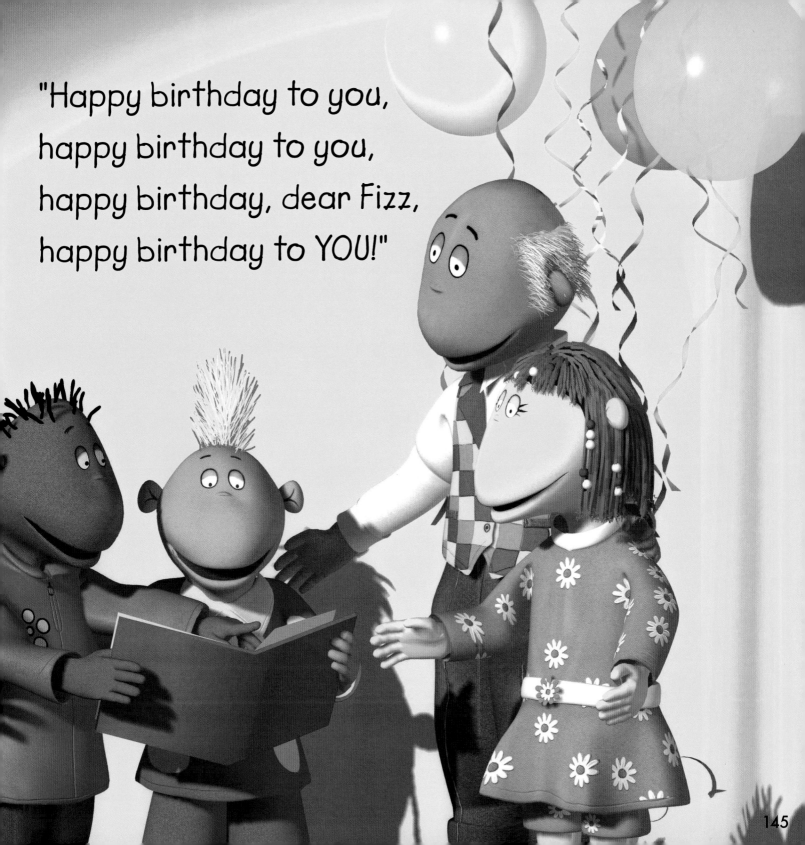

"Happy birthday to you,
happy birthday to you,
happy birthday, dear Fizz,
happy birthday to YOU!"

Fizz stared at her cake
and made a secret wish.
Then, with one big puff, she
blew out ALL the candles!

At that very moment,
Doodles raced in with
a parcel and dropped it
on the floor beside Fizz.
"WOOF WOOF!" he barked.
"Happy birthday, Fizz!"

"Thank you, Doodles!"
said Fizz. She unwrapped
the parcel and stared in
amazement at Doodle's
surprise gift.

"PINK BALLET SHOES!" she gasped. "Doodles, you've made my birthday wish come true!"

THE END

Growing Up

Little Bo hung up her rucksack on its usual peg. She noticed how easy the peg was for her to reach.

"It must be because I'm getting bigger," she thought. "After all, it is nearly time for my birthday!"

She felt sure Roly Mo would notice how grown-up she was now.

"Hello there, Little Bo," said Roly Mo.
Little Bo stood up as straight as she possibly could.
"I see you're looking very tall today," said Roly.

"I'm growing up," said Little Bo proudly. "So you are," said Roly. "Do you think you're grown-up enough to choose today's story?"

"Books over here,
books over there,
find me a book with
a story to share."

"Please may I have
a special story,
just for me," said
Little Bo.

154

When I Was One

When I Was One

It was the day before Josh's birthday. He was so excited, he couldn't talk about anything else.

"What was I like when I was one?" he asked, at breakfast.

"When you were one, you'd only just begun," said Mum. "Just like Martha."

Baby Martha was smearing jam on her face with one hand and tipping juice over the table with the other. Josh was sure he had never been so messy.

"And when I was two?" he asked, in the garden.

"You found plenty to do," said Mum. "You used to play in the mud."

The mud looked black and sticky. Josh was sure he had never wanted to play there.

"And when I was three?" he asked later.

"There was lots to see," said Mum. "You painted pictures, like this one."

Josh thought the picture was quite good.

"What will I be like when I'm five?" he asked, at bedtime.

"Wait until tomorrow," said Mum. "Then we'll find out!"

The End

"Baby Mo is my little sister, just like Martha is Josh's," said Little Bo looking at the photograph of her family on the wall.

"So she is," said Roly.

"And it's nearly my birthday, just like it was nearly Josh's," said Little Bo. "I'm getting bigger all the time!"

She dashed off to tell Yugo and Migo how grown-up she was.

"Yugo! Migo!" called Little Bo. "Where are you?"

But Yugo and Migo were too busy to talk.

"Can't stop, Little Bo!" said Yugo.

"Lots to do today!" said Migo.

"Like bouncing!"
"And snootling!"
"And hiding!"
The Snoots disappeared.
"But... but I wanted to..." said
Little Bo, getting cross. "Oh, never mind."

"Yugo and Migo are just babies,
Uncle Roly," said Little Bo. "From now on
I'm going to do grown-up things with you. Like
mending things, and reading the Daily Mole, and..."

"Listening to the radio?" said Roly. "You're just in time for my favourite gardening programme."

Little Bo sat on the sofa,
feeling excited. Listening to the
radio seemed a very grown-up thing
to do.

She watched Roly carefully, to
make sure she was doing it right.
When Roly nodded, she nodded.
When Roly chuckled, she chuckled.
When Roly fell asleep, she closed
her eyes and pretended to snore.

"Toot toot!"

Yugo and Migo popped
up beside Little Bo.

"Shhh!" she whispered.
"I'm listening to the radio
with Uncle Roly."

"The radio?" said Migo.

"Ooooeee!" said Yugo.

Little Bo began to giggle.

Roly started to wake up.

Pop! Pop! The snoots
disappeared behind
the sofa.

"Would you like to do something else grown-up now, Bo?" said Roly.

"Squeak!" squeaked Migo, behind the sofa.

"I wonder where the Snoots have got to?" said Roly, with a twinkle in his eye.

"Honk!" honked Yugo.
Then Little Bo heard a loud "Parp!"
"Uncle Roly, that was you!" she said.

"Yes, that was me!" said Roly.
"But you're grown-up," said Little Bo.
"That doesn't mean I can't make
funny noises," said Roly. "Toot toot!"
"Squeak!" squeaked Yugo.
"Honk!" honked Migo.

"Parp!" added Little Bo. "What a Roly Moly day! It doesn't matter if I'm big or small really, does it? I can still have lots of fun!"

The End

173

BBC CHILDREN'S BOOKS

Published by the Penguin Group
Penguin Books Ltd, 80 Strand, London WC2R 0RL, England
Published by BBC Children's Books, 2007
Text and design © BBC Children's Character Books, 2007
10 9 8 7 6 5 4 3 2 1
BBC and logo © and ™ BBC 1996
CBeebies & logo ™ BBC. © BBC 2002
All rights reserved.
ISBN: 978 1 405 90377 6
Printed in China

Lunar Jim
Lunar Fluffies

Text, design and illustrations © BBC Children's Character Books, 2007
Written by Iona Treahy.
Based on an original concept created by Alexander Bar
™ Alliance Atlantis. © 2005 LJ Productions 2003 Ltd./Lunar Jim Productions Inc.
Alliance Atlantis and the stylized "A" design are trademarks of Alliance Atlantis Communications Inc.
All rights reserved. Distributed by Alliance Atlantis.
First published by BBC Children's Character Books, 2007
This edition also published by BBC Children's Character Books, 2007.

Lost and Found

Text, design and illustrations © BBC Children's Character Books, 2007
Written by Iona Treahy.
Based on an original concept created by Alexander Bar
™ Alliance Atlantis. © 2005 LJ Productions 2003 Ltd./Lunar Jim Productions Inc.
Alliance Atlantis and the stylized "A" design are trademarks of Alliance Atlantis Communications Inc.
All rights reserved. Distributed by Alliance Atlantis.
First published by BBC Children's Character Books, 2007
This edition also published by BBC Children's Character Books, 2007.